Marilyn Eisenstein

Kate Can't Wait

Paintings by

Miranda Jones

Tundra Books

Published in Canada by Tundra Books, *McClelland & Stewart Young Readers*,
481 University Avenue, Toronto, Ontario M5G 2E9

Published in the United States by Tundra Books of Northern New York,
P.O. Box 1030, Plattsburgh, New York 12901

Library of Congress Control Number: 00-135455

Canadian Cataloguing in Publication Data

Eisenstein, Marilyn
    Kate can't wait

ISBN 0-88776-518-1

I. Jones, Miranda, 1955- . II. Title.

PS8559.I83K37 2001   jC813'.54   C00-932276-0
PZ7.E37Ka 2001

We acknowledge the support of the Canada Council for the Arts and the
Ontario Arts Council for our publishing program.

We acknowledge the financial support of the Government of Canada
through the Book Publishing Industry Development Program for our
publishing activities.

Medium: pen and watercolor on paper

Printed in Hong Kong, China

1 2 3 4 5 6   06 05 04 03 02 01

In loving memory of my late father,

Emil Eisenstein

M.E.

For Mama, who, at 95,

continues to nurture us all

M.J.

"Are we there yet?" Kate asked, as they drove past cloud-high buildings heading north to their new home.

"Kate Melinda Sue, good things are worth waiting for," Mother said.

Kate didn't like to wait for anything: for her hair to grow until it tickled her shoulders, for her juice to be poured, for car rides to end. . . .

She hummed an angry tune to herself and slumped down in her seat.

They drove on and on, past farms with horses and cows and endless brown fields.

"Are we there yet?" asked Kate.

"Kate Melinda Sue! This must be the fiftieth time you've asked. Good things are worth waiting for," Mother said.

Finally they turned the bend and there, on a hill, stood their farmhouse. Kate darted out of the van. "Where are the cows and the corn?" she demanded.

"We just got here, Kate, and it's early spring. You'll have to wait."

Kate didn't want to wait. She humphed and stomped across the barren field.

The next day, the doorbell rang. There stood a girl with long braids, long legs, and a long line of freckles that curved around her face like a country road. "Welcome! My name is Jessie. I live up the lane," she said.

The girls stared at each other. Kate wanted to be older like Jessie. She wanted to be taller like Jessie. She wanted to be best friends right away.

"Come over to my house tomorrow," said Jessie.

Kate couldn't wait. "How long till I can go to Jessie's house?" she asked every hour, like a gong on a grandfather clock.

"You'll just have to be patient. Good things are worth waiting for," Mother said.

"I hate to wait," muttered Kate.

Finally, the time came for Kate's visit. She loved everything about Jessie's house, especially the barn with the caramel-colored kittens curled up like balls of yarn in the basket. If only she could take home the smallest one with the softest purr....

"My mother says you can have one when they're old enough," said Jessie.

Kate couldn't wait!

"These are for you," said Jessie, when she came over the next day. She handed Kate a carton of plants, wrapped in a big red ribbon and bow.

"What are they?" asked Kate.

"They're strawberry plants," explained Jessie.

With a bewildered look, Kate plunked them on the wooden table. "I don't see any strawberries," she said.

"Wait and see," said Jessie.

"I don't want to wait," grumbled Kate.

"Come on, Jessie, let's play on the swing," Kate suggested.

"We should plant these first," said Jessie. "Dig in." She showed Kate how to place the strawberry plants gently into the ground.

Kate thought about the juicy red strawberries she had seen at Katz's fruit stand, just around the corner from her old apartment. "Why can't we just buy them?" she asked.

"They'll be delicious. Wait and see."

But Kate didn't want to wait.

Every morning Kate visited her little garden, but nothing seemed to change. "Be strawberries already!" Kate yelled.

Slowly, slowly the plants got bigger and tiny buds appeared. But still no strawberries.

"Grow, grow, grow," she hollered, kicking her rubber shoe at the plants.

Kate almost forgot about the strawberry plants. Then, one sunny day, when the buttercups covered the wide-open fields like a soft yellow blanket, she noticed that her strawberry plants were drooping.

"What's happening?" she cried to her mother.

"You can't just wait for them to grow, Kate. You have to help them."

Every morning, from then on, Kate plopped her wide straw hat on her head and watered the plants with her yellow watering can. At first, white flowers bloomed. Then the petals dropped. And soon the first small green strawberries appeared. When Kate wasn't looking, squirrels, rabbits, and birds came along and ate some.

"Please don't die," Kate pleaded softly to her plants. She patted them as if they were the small kittens at Jessie's house, and whispered lovingly, "You are my strawberries, small and sweet. You are everybody's favorite treat."

Kate and Jessie watered the plants and watched the strawberries grow and grow. Slowly the berries turned white, pink, and finally, bright shiny red. Now they were ready to be picked!

The girls plucked the strawberries from their stems one by one and carefully placed them in a straw basket, as if they were rubies.

That afternoon, Kate and Jessie gave a tea party with a big bowl of juicy red strawberries and fresh cream.

"Kate Melinda Sue, these are the sweetest strawberries I've ever tasted," Mother exclaimed.

"Some things are just worth waiting for," Kate said.